T0196946

HAPPY PARENTING: HAPPY KIDS

HAPPY PARENTING: HAPPY KIDS

THE PARENT'S MANUAL

JOAN D. ATWOOD, Ph.D.
&
AMANDEEP GEENA GARHA, M.S

HAPPY PARENTING: HAPPY KIDS
THE PARENT'S MANUAL

iUniverse books may be ordered through booksellers or by contacting:

iUniverse
1663 Liberty Drive
Bloomington, IN 47403
www.iuniverse.com
1-800-Authors (1-800-288-4677)

ISBN: 978-1-5320-5466-2 (sc)
ISBN: 978-1-5320-5558-4 (e)

Print information available on the last page.

iUniverse rev. date: 08/21/2018

ESTABLISHING POSITIVE RELATIONS WITH YOUR CHILDREN

Philosophy

The E.S.P (Enhancing Skills for Parents) Program supports the idea that the most challenging role in society today is that of being a parent. Yet, there are few, if any, educational programs that help parents develop the attributes necessary to meet the needs of this role. It is also apparent that traditional methods of raising children are no longer as effective as they were a generation ago. E.S.P. provides parents with realistic and practical methods for meeting the challenges of raising children today. E.S.P. offers a safe, supportive environment where parents become actively involved in discussing common concerns, while learning effective, enjoyable ways to relate to their children. Parents develop increased confidence and learn to maximize their potentials skills in order to create more satisfying and more productive relationships with their children.

While many specific topics are covered, the overall goal of the E.S.P. program is twofold:

1. To improve and enhance parent-child relationships
2. To help parents learn the skills necessary to raise responsible children who will grow into responsible adults capable of living meaningful, happy lives.
3. To help parents experience happy parenting rather than

Specific Objectives for the E.S.P. Program:

1. Participants identify, acknowledge, and use emotions to build positive relationships with their children.

2. Participants utilize emotions to improve communication and listening skills.

3. Participants examine the effects of biases, perceptions, appraisal processes, and possible self fulfilling prophecies on parent-child relationships.

4. Participants learn to use encouragement and to be optimistic in their expectations of their children.

5. Participants increase understanding and develop realistic expectations from knowledge of children's developmental issues.

6. Participants increase awareness of the role of emotions in implementing effective discipline.

7. Participants learn various approaches to discipline to foster cooperation and avoid daily battles with their children.

8. Participants develop skills for resolving conflicts and exploring alternatives with their children.

9. Participants learn methods for developing responsibility and cooperation in their children.

10. Participants explore and develop alternative scripts to deal with both their anger and their children's anger.

11. Facilitators identify topics related to parenting issues which are of interest to participants.

12. Facilitators survey participants upon completion of the program to ascertain the usefulness of the program.

Guidelines for Participants in the E.S.P. Program

Participants are responsible to be respectful to themselves and to other participants. Therefore, we encourage all members to freely contribute to group discussions and maintain the highest level of respect when others are contributing as well. To reinforce this, we maintain the following guidelines:

✓ **NO CROSS-TALK**: Do not speak while others are speaking. There should not be any side conversations among other group members when another participant is sharing.

✓ **"I" STATEMENTS**: Participants are directed to use "I" statements when answering others in the room. Remember to talk about your <u>own</u> experience.

- ✓ **OFFER SUPPORTIVE ADVICE**: Give statements that reinforce positive growth for each other.

- ✓ **NON-JUDGMENTAL ACCEPTANCE OF OTHER PARTICIPANTS VIEWPOINTS**: Do not judge or blame others, it is important to suspend individual value judgments, and encourage one another to safely explore experiences that may not generally be accepted.

- ✓ **MAINTAIN CONTINUITY AND COMMITMENT**: Arrive on time and attend every session. Participants are asked to commit to all of the program's sessions and to arrive promptly so that the group can begin on time.

BUILDING MY HOME

- ✓ The <u>foundation</u>: Write the beliefs that govern your life.

- ✓ The <u>walls</u>*:* Write methods you use to strengthen these beliefs in your family.

- ✓ The <u>roof</u>: How do you protect or defend you values?

- ✓ The <u>window</u>: Write something about your family values that you are proud of.

- ✓ The <u>door</u>: If someone entered your home, what would they notice that gives them clues about your values?

PERSONAL DEVELOPMENT EXERCISE

ENCOURAGEMENT:

1. Take an inventory of your assets: What are the things you like about the way you relate with your child/children. Recognize positive aspects of the relationship. List at least five things.

2. How can you use these assets to further improve the way you relate to your child/children?

3. What are the things you like about your child/children? Recognize positive traits and consider alternatives to what may appear to be negative traits. List at least five things.

4. How can you focus on these assets and become a more encouraging parent? Make some specific plans:

UNDERSTANDING MORE ABOUT YOUR CHILD AND ABOUT YOURSELF AS A PARENT

Emotions:

Typically, we regard emotions as magical forces which invade us from the outside. We seem not to realize that each of us is responsible for her or his own emotions. Our emotions are based on our beliefs and purposes. ***We feel as we believe.***

Parents often become annoyed and angry with children because the children will not do what the parents want them to. These hostile feelings of anger and annoyance serve the purpose of controlling the children. Once parents decide that they do not need to be controlling (that they can set limits and let the children decide and learn from the consequences), then there is no purpose for becoming annoyed and angry.

Children learn to use their emotions to achieve goals as well. Once parents recognize how children can use emotions to achieve goals, parents are in a position to influence their children.

We know that becoming responsible for one's own feelings is a necessary part of growing—and becoming an effective parent.

Adapted from Dinkmeyer & McKay Copyright © 1989

Lifestyle:

We develop beliefs about who we are, who and what other people are, what is important in life, and how we should function so that we can belong. We live by our beliefs; they characterize our *lifestyle.*

Yet, our basic beliefs are often faulty. Why? Because our interpretations of our experiences are often inaccurate. We formed our most basic beliefs when we were very young. At hat time our limited experience caused us to misjudge and overgeneralize.

It is important to understand the factors that influence the formation of our children's lifestyle. The four major factors that contribute to the formation of the children's lifestyle are:

1. ***Family atmosphere and values:***

   The patterns in the human relationships set by parents are called the "family atmosphere." The atmosphere may be:

   - Competitive or cooperative
   - Friendly or hostile

- Autocratic or permissive
- Orderly or chaotic

2. ***Family values:***

Family values can be easily recognizable (valuing religion, education, hard work), while others may not be as obvious (valuing power, control, winning, being right). Share interests reflect the family values. Children cannot remain neutral about the values their family holds. Each child must decide which and how much of the values of the family to adopt as their own.

3. ***Sex roles:***

The sex roles played by parents are guidelines for their children. Children base their attitudes toward their own sex and the opposite sex on their observations of their parents. They may accept or reject the models their parents present.

Adapted from Dinkmeyer & McKay Copyright © 1989

4. ***Birth order:***

The psychological position of a child in a family is often related to the child's position among siblings. Each child has a different position in the family and perceives all events from her or his own viewpoint. Each position tends to have its own characteristic line of development and related beliefs and attitudes. It is important to recognize that these positions in the family constellation only influence an individual's personality development; they do not directly determine it. Each individual makes his or her own decisions.

5. ***Methods of training:***

Parents' attitudes and behavior toward children and toward themselves influences children's lifestyle. A parent may be autocratic or permissive or inconsistent in their behavior towards their children, and this is greatly influenced by how they were reared. A parent's lifestyle growing up influences his or her present behavior as parents. However, the results of our training are not always what we expect, because it is the child, not the parents, who decides how the child will respond.

It is in response to these four major influences (family atmosphere and values, sex roles, birth order, and methods of training) that children develop their convictions and long-range goals. If they are able to meet their immediate goals through constructive acts, they become cooperative children. If, however, they find that they cannot achieve their goals constructively, they may become discouraged children who feel they must misbehave to secure a place in life.

THE FOUR BASIC INGREDIENTS FOR BUILDING POSITIVE RELATIONSHIPS

1. Mutual Respect:

Respect is earned; it comes from showing respect to others. To establish mutual respect, we must be willing to demonstrate respect for our children.

- ✓ Minimize negative talk.
- ✓ Talk with your children when the atmosphere is calm.

2. Encouragement:

We must believe in our children if they are to believe in themselves.

- ✓ Minimize the importance of your children's mistakes.
- ✓ Recognize their assets and strengths.

3. Communicating Love:

To feel secure, each child must have at least one significant person to love and to be loved by.

- ✓ Tell your children you love them when they are not anticipating it.
- ✓ Nonverbal signs such as pats, hugs, kisses, and tousling hair are extremely important.

4. Spending Time Together:

The important ingredient of time together is ***quality*** not quantity. An hour of positive relationship is worth more than several hours of conflict.

- ✓ Spend time each day with each child doing something you **both** enjoy.
- ✓ Agree on the time. Plan the activity together. Do not allow interruptions.
- ✓ Keep it simple. Keep it consistent. Follow through.

UNDERSTANDING BEHAVIOR

Behavior occurs for a social purpose. People are decision-making social beings whose main goal in life is to belong. In our search, we select beliefs, feelings and behavior which we feel will gain us significance. Behavior can best be understood by observing its consequences.

- ✓ Observe your own reaction to the child's misbehavior. *Your feelings* point to the child's goals.
- ✓ Observe the child's response to your attempts at correction. *The child's response to your behavior* will also let you know what the child is after.
- ✓ Train yourself to look at the results of misbehavior rather than just at the misbehavior.
- ✓ The results of the misbehavior reveal its purpose.

All misbehavior stems from discouragement. The child lacks the courage to behave in an active, constructive manner. A child may use misbehavior for different goals or misbehave in different ways to achieve the same purpose.

NOTE: Children are often aware of the consequences of their misbehavior, but they are usually unaware of their goals.

Points to remember when trying to understand behavior:

- ✓ Effective parenting requires patience.
- ✓ Effective parenting requires active attendance and awareness.
- ✓ All behavior has a social purpose.
- ✓ Responsible children are influenced by responsible parents.
- ✓ Focus on the child's assets and strength, rather than on finding fault.
- ✓ Showing confidence in the child will help the child develop self-confidence.

THE FOUR GOALS OF MISBEHAVIOR

Attention:

Children prefer to gain attention through useful ways but will seek attention in useless ways if that is the only way they can get attention. Children who hold the conviction that they can belong only if they are receiving attention prefer negative attention to being ignored.

- ✓ Focus on constructive behavior.
- ✓ Ignore misbehavior or pay attention to it in ways the child does not expect.
- ✓ Attention should not be given on demand, even for positive acts.
- ✓ Give attention when it is not expected. This changes the emphasis from 'getting attention' to being 'given attention.'

Power:

Power-seeking children feel they are significant only when they are boss. Some children in power struggles do what they are told, but not in a way the parents want it done (defiant compliance).

- ✓ Refrain from getting angry.
- ✓ Disengage from the power struggle.
- ✓ Do not use power tactics to counter children's bids for power. This only impresses them with the value of power and increases their desire for it.

Revenge:

Children who pursue revenge believe they are significant only when they are hurting others as they believe they have been hurt. They find a place by being cruel and disliked.

- ✓ Do not retaliate.
- ✓ Remain calm and show good will.

Display of inadequacy:

Children who display inadequacy, or disability, are *extremely* discouraged. They have given up hope of succeeding. They attempt to keep others from expecting anything of them. Giving up may be total or only in areas where children feel they can't succeed.

- ✓ Eliminate all criticism.
- ✓ Focus on the child's assets and strengths.
- ✓ Encourage any effort to improve, no matter how small it seems.

Points to remember when trying to understand behavior:

- ✓ Your reactions and feelings about a child's misbehavior point to the purpose of that behavior.
- ✓ The child's behavior can most effectively be influenced by changing your own behavior.
- ✓ When the child is misbehaving, do what he or she does not expect, that is consider doing exactly the opposite from what you would typically do.
- ✓ Show appreciation for the child's positive behaviors, unless they are meant only to gain attention.
- ✓ Withdraw from power struggles.
- ✓ Because retaliation stimulates further revenge, do not retaliate. Express good will to improve the quality of the relationship.

- ✓ A child who seeks power often has a parent who likes to boss others.
- ✓ A child who displays inadequacy is not unable; rather, the child lacks belief in his or her ability.

Adapted from Dinkmeyer & McKay Copyright © 1989

GOALS OF POSITIVE BEHAVIOR

ATTENTION/INVOLVEMENT/CONTRIBUTION:

- Child's belief: "I belong by contributing."
- Behavior: Helps. Volunteers.
- How to encourage positive goals: Let child know the contribution counts and that you appreciate it.

POWER/AUTONOMY/RESPONSIBILITY FOR OWN BEHAVIOR:

- Child's belief: "I can decide and be responsible for my behavior."
- Behavior: Shows self discipline. Does own work. Is resourceful.

- How to encourage positive goals: Encourage child's decision making. Let child experience both positive and negative outcomes. Express confidence in child.

Justice/Fairness:

- Child's belief: "I am interested in cooperating."
- Behavior: Returns kindness for hurt. Ignores belittling comments.
- How to encourage positive goals: Let child know you appreciate her or his interest in cooperating.

Withdrawal from conflict/Refusal to fight/ Acceptance of others' opinions:

- Child's belief: "I can decide to withdraw from conflict."
- Behavior: Ignores provocations. Withdraws from power contest to decide own behavior.
- How to encourage positive goals: Recognize child's effort to act maturely.

Adapted from Dinkmeyer & McKay Copyright © 1989

POINTS TO REMEMBER:

Temperament and the Developmental Stages of Children

1. Each child is born with an individual temperament. Accept a child's temperament and build on it.

2. Each child goes through stages of development at an individual rate and in a particular style.

3. Each developmental stage has proposed tasks that children master when they are ready. For example:

✓ Infant: task is to learn to trust other humans, themselves, and the world around them

✓ Toddler: task is to experiment with independence

✓ Preschooler: tasks are to create their own worlds, practice adult roles, play with language, and learn to get along with other children

4. Children often sense parents' expectations of them and react as expected.

5. To enhance parenting, find and create opportunities to say "***yes***" rather than "NO."

6. Help children to respect themselves and others. Encouraging children's positive beliefs about themselves can lead to positive behavior patterns.

7. Allow children time to play. Play is their work, and they must do it to develop and grow.

8. Provide freedom within limits. A democratic family atmosphere builds responsibility and teaches children respect for themselves and others.

ENCOURAGEMENT A WAY TO DEVELOP A CHILD'S POTENTIAL

The language of encouragement avoids value judgments by eliminating words like good, great and terrific. Instead, it focuses on the individual's strengths, conveys a message of confidence in the individual, and helps promote high self-esteem.

Phrases that demonstrate acceptance:

"I like the way you handled that."

"I'm glad you enjoyed yourself."

"How do you feel about this?

Phrases that show confidence:

"You'll make it."

"You're making progress."

"I believe you'll handle it."

Phrases that recognize effort and improvement:

"I can see you put a lot of effort into that."

"I can see a lot of progress."

"You're improving in ________________."

Strategies for Encouraging:

1. Give responsibility.
2. Show appreciation for efforts made to help the household function smoothly.
3. Ask for opinions and suggestions.
4. Encourage participation in decision making.
5. Accept mistakes.
6. Emphasize the process, not the product.
7. Focus on the child's strengths and assets, not on his or her faults.
8. Show confidence in your child's judgment.
9. Have positive expectations.
10. Develop alternative ways of viewing situations.

THE RIGHTS OF PARENTS AND CHILDREN

Oftentimes parents may see themselves as all-sacrificing for their children. This attitude is stressful for parents and unhealthy for children. Children who grow up feeling they have to be the center of the universe may have problems in relationships. Consider the rights listed below. They can be summed up in one phrase: the right to mutual respect.

Parents have the right to:

- ✓ Live their lives apart from their children.
- ✓ Time for themselves and adult relationships.
- ✓ Friendships with others.
- ✓ Privacy.
- ✓ Have their property respected.

Children have the right to:

- ✓ Be raised in a loving, safe atmosphere.
- ✓ Have their wishes considered.
- ✓ Be respected as a unique individual.
- ✓ A life apart from being the child in the family.
- ✓ Privacy.
- ✓ Have their property respected.

What will you do this week to maintain your rights?

How will you show respect for your child's rights?

THE FAMILY LIFE CYCLE

Most of us are familiar with the family life cycle. Even young children are acquainted with the life cycle, singing schoolyard rhymes about love, marriage, and a baby carriage. Each life cycle stage has tasks that must be achieved to move successfully to the next stage, along with stage-specific issues and changes that we may encounter.

Types of Problems Found in the Family Life Cycle:

- Normal Stage specific difficulties
- Maladaptive responses to the specific pressures of a given stage
- Chronic problems related to unresolved issues from a prior developmental stage or stages

Two Kinds of Stressors in Families:

Horizontal Stressors:

These stressors correspond to the crises associated with the family's movement through the life cycle.

Ex. Birth of a child, Accidental death of a child, Teenager gets pregnant

Vertical Stressors:

These stressors include patterns of relating and functioning that are transmitted across generations.

Ex. The legacies and missions handed down through the generations

Changes Occur at Different Levels:

- ✓ Changes at the Individual Level
- ✓ Changes at the Systemic Level
- ✓ Changes at the Relational Ethics Level

STAGE I

The Family Life Cycle

MARRIAGE

Two separate individuals must establish a new unit: *the couple.* As they come together, they must establish reasonable boundaries with their families of origin.

The Major Tasks At This Stage are related to both partners moving away from families of origin and toward one another.

Moving Beyond Attraction:

Trust, Commitment, and Relationship Turning Points

- Trust refers to the belief that one's partner will not exploit or take unfair advantage of his or her.
- Commitment is reflected in the degree to which we are willing to work for the continuation of the relationship, and it is in this willingness to work for the relationship that distinguishes an

increasingly intimate and exclusive relationship from one that is casual and unchanging.

- Turning Points: A relationship goes through critical periods or turning points. This is when a relationship either evolves to a deeper level of intimacy and involvement or dissolves.

Gay and Lesbian Marriage

- It is estimated that 1% of adult women self identify as lesbian and 2% of men identify as gay.
- It is estimated that 50% of gay women and 40% of gay men between the ages of 18-59 are currently living with a same sex partner.
- 60% of heterosexuals are living with a partner.
- The experience of these couples is more similar than different to heterosexual couples.

***ATTACHMENT*:** Attachment Theory (Bowlby) implies that the capacity to form emotional attachments to others is primarily developed during infancy and early childhood.

Three Distinct Attachment Patterns:

- ✓ **Secure**-when parents are responsive to a child, the child will become securely attached and be less inhibitive and exhibit more exploratory behavior.
- ✓ **Avoidant**- Constantly ignoring or deflecting the needs and the attention of the child leads to Avoidant Attachment style in which the child attempts to maintain proximity but avoids close contact with the caregiver.
- ✓ **Anxious**-Ambivalent- When a parent s inconsistent in responding and attention giving, the child has an anxious ambivalent attachment that tries to re-establish contact, clings to the caregiver, and constantly looks to see where the caregiver is.

TASKS

At the Individual Level:

- ✓ Both partners have to look less to their families of origin and more toward each other for meeting basic emotional needs such as caring, comfort, company, and support.

Developmental Tasks of the Married Couple Include:

- ✓ Establishing an Identity as a Married Couple.
- ✓ Establishing Marital Themes
- ✓ Negotiating Marital Roles
- ✓ Evolving a Congruence of Conjugal Identities
- ✓ Regulating Distances Between Family and Friends
- ✓ Managing the Household
- ✓ Managing the Emotional Climate of the Relationship
- ✓ Evolving a Marital Sexual Script
- ✓ Managing Conflict

At the Systemic Level:

- ✓ Both partners have to establish a series of ground rules and patterns that allow them to function well as a couple.

At the Relational Ethical Level:

- ✓ The central task involves both partners' efforts to balance loyalties to their families of origin, their new partners and themselves.

PROBLEMS

Typical Problems at This Stage Include:

- o Chronic Arguing
- o Constant tension and "walking on eggshells."
- o Difficulties setting ground rules or resolving conflicts.
- o Complaints of selfishness, unavailability, or demanding
- o Having a hard time balancing loyalties between family of origin and marital relationship.
    - o "I'm going home to mother" syndrome.
- o Family Cutoffs. Cutting off family of origin.
    - o This is also a problem of boundaries.

THINKING QUESTIONS:

Mate Section:

Theorists have different opinions regarding mate selection: Basically they hold two opposite views: birds of a feather flock together or opposites attract. In you're your opinion, which do you believe is the case and why?

Couples therapists believe that when a couple come together they "know" right away whether there is a "click" or not. They also believe that this click is an unconscious recognition that this person is a "soulmate." There is some anecdotal evidence that suggests this might be the case in that if you ask married couples how they knew this was the person they wanted to marry, they say, "I just knew." I had one husband say to me, "As soon as I saw her, I knew I would marry her. I didn't care if she was an ax murderer, I knew we would be together!" In your opinion, discuss why or why not this theory is true and why.

Getting Married:

People say that marriage ruins a good sex life. In your opinion, is this true or not true and why? Think about the pluses and minuses involved in the institution of marriage.

STAGE II

Birth Of The Children

The birth of children has a sweeping impact on the lives of the two new parents.

The major task is to attempt to integrate their relationship that already exists between the two of them. They have to integrate the parental subsystem into the couple.

TASKS

At the Individual Level:

- ✓ Increased Level of Physical and Emotional Demands Placed on Two People
- ✓ Responsibility for Caring for the New Baby
- ✓ New Skills are Needed
- ✓ Individual Identities are Changed:
    - o Positive- New Meaning to Life
    - o Negative- Parents Feel Inadequate

At the Systemic Level:

- ✓ This means the creation of new boundaries, subsystems and roles.
- ✓ The marital subsystem must make room for the parental subsystem.
- ✓ The boundaries they create will regulate the coexistence of these subsystems within the new family. Ex. Child having his or her own room.

At the Relational Ethics Level:

- ✓ The basic task involves both parents efforts to balance their increasingly complex networks of obligation and entitlement—at this point, obligations to one's child, one's spouse, one's family of origin and one's self.

Other Developmental Tasks Accompanying Parenthood:

- ✓ Altering Family Themes
- ✓ Defining a Parental Role Identity
- ✓ The Child's Evolving Identity
- ✓ Renegotiating Distances With Family and Friends
- ✓ Realigning Marital Boundaries

- ✓ Balancing the Boundary Between Work and Family
- ✓ Making a Family Household
- ✓ Managing Finances
- ✓ Maintaining the Couple Relationship
- ✓ Maintaining a Satisfying Sexual Relationship
- ✓ Managing Leisure Activities
- ✓ Managing New Areas of Conflict

PROBLEMS

Typical Problems:

- One is overinvolved with the child
- Decreased marital satisfaction
- Depressed and/or overwhelmed
- Insufficient involvement with the child
- Intense, stormy marital relationship

THINKING QUESTIONS:

Marriage and Young Children:

And baby makes three. First the first time, there is a triangle. Becoming a couple and becoming parents are the activities of people in their twenties and thirties. The trap here is that the couple loses the couple and they start relating to each other as parents and nothing more. What precautions can couples take to safeguard against this?

Divorce:

Some people say that Divorce should be a stage in the "normal" life cycle because the majority of people get divorced in US society (57% in NYS). Do you agree or disagree with this statement? If you choose at some point in your life to divorce, what protections can you make for yourself and/or your children?

STAGE III

Elementary School

INDIVIDUATION OF THE CHILDREN

This stage starts when the child is two.

There are two aspects:

1. Beginning social activity outside the home, with peers and adults, at school or play.

2. Involves natural evolution of parental expectations regarding the child, which coincides with the child's developing readiness for such expectations.

TASKS

The Major Tasks are Twofold:

- ✓ Trying to balance the growing autonomy of the child with his or her sense of belonging and loyalty to the family, without either "binding" or "expelling" the child.
- ✓ Trying to maintain a reasonable and fair balance of accountability between parents and child, without either overburdening the child with expectations and missions or expecting too little or nothing of the child.

The Individual Level:

- ✓ Parents must face what may be their first sense of psychological separation from the child.
- ✓ They may experience increased fears concerning the child's welfare out of the house, out of sight, as well as concern over the kinds of influence to which the child will be exposed.
- ✓ The child may face fears associated with the world outside or fears of being separated from parents, etc.
- ✓ The child has to begin to consider how to balance his or her own needs and desires with those of other children as well as with their parents.
- ✓ The child begins to develop a need and capacity to contribute, to be of help in some way, especially to his or her parents and other family members.

The Systemic Level:

- ✓ The boundaries between and around the child and the parents are significantly changed at this point.
- ✓ The child becomes involved in systems outside the family, such as friendships with peers and school.
- ✓ The child begins to spend more time away from home and parents.
- ✓ The boundaries between child and parents become firmer than they previously have been.
- ✓ The clarity and flexibility of these boundaries between these systems become increasingly important as the child grows older.
- ✓ If there are two or more children, the sibling subsystem is created.
- ✓ As the children become less involved with parents, the necessity of maintaining boundaries between generations and of balancing marital and parental obligations continues.

The Relational Ethical Level:

- ✓ The child may begin to take on missions and with them roles which can exert a major influence on his or future life.
- ✓ These could be missions to care for one or both parents for their marriage, for the family as a whole or to achieve and reflect pride toward the family. All these may become noticeable at this time.
- ✓ These missions may or may not be harmful to the child depending on the flexibility of the parents.

Questions for Parents to Explore:

Is too much being asked of the child?
Is the child being asked to put aside their own
needs in order to help others in the family?
Is merit of the child's contributions being acknowledged?
Is too little being expected of the child?
Does the child contribute anything?
Does s/he give too much, too little?

Four Parenting Styles:

- **The Indulgent Parents:**
  - Indulgent Parents are referred to as permissive or non-directive, as responsive but not demanding. They avoid confrontation.
    - **Two Types:**
      - **Democratic** are more conscientious, engaged, and committed to the children
      - **Non-Directive** Parents are much more laid back in their approach.

- **The Authoritarian Parents:**
  - Authoritarian parents are highly demanding and directive, but not responsive. They are obedience and status oriented and expect their orders to be obeyed without explanation. These parents want to curb the child's self will. They use punitive and forceful methods to accomplish this.

- **The Authoritative Parents:**
  - The Authoritative Parents are both demanding and responsive. They impart clear standards fir their children and are assertive but nor intrusive and restrictive.

- **The Uninvolved Parents:**
  - Uninvolved parents are low I both responsiveness and demandingness. These parents can be thought of as both neglectful and permissive. Children are given no clear rules for behavior and they receive little or no attention. This type of parenting can leave children anxious, confused, and unable to internalize standards for self-control.

PROBLEMS

Common Problems:

- Families having problems at this stage usually present the child in therapy as the identified patient.
  - The one exception is the single parent who presents with depression, anxiety, loneliness, when the child starts school. Very often s/he feels unemployed.
- Usually though the problem is defined as relational, that is, they define it as a problem between parents and child.
- **School Phobia**. It is common for the child to want to stay home or not want to go to school. Here the child could be afraid of school or what is called a fear could reflect loyalty

and responsibility on the part of the child for the parent in the home. It could also reflect the family member not being able to tolerate the absence of the child.

- Child could have **enuresis** and/or **encopresis**.
- Child could refuse to be separated from her doll.
- Child could develop a psychosomatic disorder such as asthma or stomach aches.
- Child may act stubborn, rebellious, or selfish.
- Child may have **temper tantrums**. This usually reflects a child who is not held accountable enough by parents. It could also reflect a child whom little is expected by parents, much is allowed, and discipline is inconsistent or near existent.
- These children are paradoxically deprived. They are deprived of learning about those aspects of reality such as needs, feelings, and rights of others, which would result in the child to put limits on their own behaviors, needs and expectations. Without any effective counterbalance, these needs go unchecked.
- The result is that the natural limitations may begin to feel unreasonable to these children.

STAGE IV

Individuation Of The Adolescents

THE WONDER YEARS

Puberty signals the beginning of this stage. Physical and psychological changes disrupt structural patterns that had evolved between the parent and the child.

Central task for the family is to redefine the terms of the parent- child relationship. This is primarily regarding issues of autonomy, responsibility, and control without fundamentally violating their basic trustworthiness.

The child is in limbo— not a child, not an adult.

TASKS

The Individual Psychological Level

- ✓ Parents face a loss of control over the now adolescent son/ daughter.
- ✓ Parents may be faced for the first time with overt rebellion.

- ✓ Parents are confronted with the child's development of sexual maturity.
- ✓ Parents may feel as though they are losing their child.
- ✓ For the teenagers, there is a loss of play.
- ✓ There is a loss of special exemptions because they are children.
- ✓ They are confronted with the tasks of adulthood.
- ✓ There are increased responsibilities.
- ✓ They are expected to work- to get a driver's license.
- ✓ There are issues of sexuality, identity, and peer group relations.

The Systemic Level

- ✓ Fundamental change involves strengthening of boundaries between parents and adolescents.
- ✓ Clearly expressed in adolescent's room.
- ✓ Teenager's participation in the system of the family begins to be more evenly balanced by participation in the system of peers outside the home.

The Relational Ethical Level

- ✓ As the teenager begins to develop a more separate autonomous self apart from the family, s/he necessarily becomes more involved in developing his other identity as a separate, individual person.
- ✓ The efforts to balance loyalties to self and to others in the family necessarily become complex.
- ✓ Parents may feel under appreciated or shortchanged. Parents may experience doubts about trusting adolescents.
- ✓ From the adolescent side, trust of parents is often endangered by the imposition of parental decisions or rules.
- ✓ The parents may feel ambivalent. Parents are torn between the urge to hold onto the child and to see him or her group and away. Similarly, the adolescent may be torn between urges to grow out of the family and to remain in it as a child.

- ✓ The adolescent may begin to take on certain missions of the family. These are important that they may influence what Erikson has called the search for identity.
- ✓ Teen may feel expected to carry on the family traditions. May bear a strong legacy to achieve or succeed in some way to reflect pride on family or the opposite, to fail so as not to surpass a parent's level of achievement.

PROBLEMS

Common Problems:

- o Rebellious acting out adolescent, such as poor grades in school, truancy, experiencing with drugs, running away from home.
- o The second problem usually involves not the adolescent who is struggling for freedom but the opposite case— one who is tied to parents.

Individuation

- o It is important for the young adults to feel psychologically free from their parent's control.
- o It is crucially important for parent's to work as a team during this stage—to be on the same page.

Main Task is to safely create a departure from the home

THINKING QUESTION:

Parents of Teenagers:

One of my clients said that living with teenagers was like oral surgery without Novocain, like a thousand paper cuts or like Debby Boone singing "You light up my life" over and over. What did he mean by this? Are there issues that arise that are unique for parents of teenagers? What are they? How can teenagers bring joy to a marriage? Stress to a marriage? What were the issues you faced when you were a teenager?

STAGE V

Departure Of The Children

The main task is to separate without breaking ties. Families need to balance a dual commitment.

TASKS

The Individual Psychological Level

- ✓ Parents are faced with the loss of the child as a focus in their daily lives.

The Empty Nest Syndrome

- ✓ In most families there is some sort of preparation since the child has been growing more independent.
- ✓ The young person may face unfamiliarity of living alone, loneliness or homesickness and/or a sense of not fitting in.
- ✓ They are forced to accept responsibility

The Systemic Level

- ✓ Departure of the child involves a major change in the boundaries within the family.
- ✓ Change in the physical boundaries occurs- - the child is outside of the home.
- ✓ When the child develops a couple's relationship, there is another change in the structure to accommodate the "in-law."
- ✓ If there are any younger children at home, they get promoted to the rank of oldest child.

Three Modes of Separation Between Parents and Adolescents

- **The Binding Mode**
    - Here the child is unable to leave home. These bound young adults remain in the house, often out of a mixture of concerns for and an attachment to the family and fears of facing stressful aspects of independent living.

- **The Delegating Mode**
    - Here the child is sent out of the family but with some kind of mission to accomplish. They are permitted to leave home but they are held responsible by themselves as well as others in the family to pursue the missions called for by the family structure and history.

- **The Expelling Mode**
    - Here the child is spit out of the family with no missions to fulfill. They are permitted to leave, forced to leave with little sense that they are either wanted or needed by the family.

The Relational Ethics Level

- ✓ Does the child have a right to leave home?
- ✓ Is the child entitled to have a life of his or her own?
- ✓ Like the young adult, parents are trying to balance their dual commitments to the grown child, to themselves, and to each other.
- ✓ The parent child relationship at this point clearly becomes a two way street.

PROBLEMS

Common Problems:

- Exaggeration of some aspect of the separation process.
- Some adult children remain at home indefinitely.
- Some adult children are kicked out of the house.
- The young adult repeatedly fails to live alone.

- Feelings of isolation—not fitting in new job—anxiety, despair.
- Marital complaints
- As with each of the earlier stages, the poorer the resolution of an earlier stage, the more difficult the tasks of the following stage will become. The better the resolution of this particular stage, the better prepared the family will be for the last stage.

THINKING QUESTIONS:

The Quarterlife Crisis:

Discuss what you see as contributing to the Quarterlife Crisis. The quarterlife crisis refers to what seems to be the mini crises occurring in 20 somethings. I have posted an article I wrote that explains it in more detail. Think about this crisis from a social and historical framework. Present personal information (from acquaintances/friends/relatives/or yourself if you choose) that you have heard or observed that relates to this new phenomenon.

Menopause:

Hot flashes, depression, homicidal and suicidal feelings—these are but a few of the symptoms that young women are taught about menopause. Are they true—not true? Can they be compared to PMS? Is there such a thing as PMS? What are the effects? How do you think these life cycle events effect relationships? There is a paper posted regarding this topic as well.

Late Adulthood:

Some people say they have abandonment fears; some people say they have abandonment fantasies. What does this refer to, in your opinion?

STAGE VI

Aging And Death Of The Parents

The basic task involves facing and accepting a variety of losses.

The family's task is to face and accept these losses without significantly damaging the basic level of trustworthiness, which has been built up in these relationships.

LOSSES

Relational Losses. There are the parent's losses of friends, the survivor's loss of a spouse, the children's loss of parents.

Physical Losses. There are possible health losses as person's age, vocational losses in retirement and possibly financial losses.

TASKS

The Individual Psychological Level

- ✓ If not working, the individual may feel some loss of self esteem, self worth.
- ✓ They may feel as though they are no longer making a contribution.
- ✓ They may miss the activity, the social life.
- ✓ They may feel unwanted— as though they have been put out to pasture.
- ✓ As old age progresses, they must cope with a gradual diminishing of physical strength. They may have difficulty hearing, seeing, etc.
- ✓ These physical losses may affect a person's ego integrity.
- ✓ Each person faces his or her own death, his or her own accomplishments, failures, regrets, and satisfactions. They might experience increased stress, irritability. They may complain.
- ✓ As old age progresses, they must cope with a gradual diminishing of physical strength. They may have difficulty hearing, seeing, etc.
- ✓ These physical losses may affect a person's ego integrity.
- ✓ Each person faces his or her own death, his or her own accomplishments, failures, regrets, and satisfactions.
- ✓ They might experience increased stress, irritability. They may complain.

The Systemic Level

- ✓ The adult child and the parent may become afraid.

The Relational Ethical Level

- ✓ Both the dying person and the survivor may ask themselves if they did enough for each other.
- ✓ They may wish that they had done more or that they could undo certain things.
- ✓ They may wish that they could make up for certain things.
- ✓ They may ask for forgiveness.
- ✓ It is important that the adult children beguiled by some notion of realistic accountability in weighing how much they can give and in what ways.

PROBLEMS

Common Problems

- o If the parent is ill, the spouse may present with symptoms of anxiety and/or depression.
- o If the parent dies, there is a grief reaction for the adult child.
- o If the spouse dies, there is a grief reaction for the missed partner.
- o If the parent lives with the adult child, either can present with complaints.
- o The spouse of the adult child may have complaints.
- o A couple who have regulated distance in the marriage by triangulating in the parent may need to substitute a different third party (a lover, a child, a bottle, a therapist

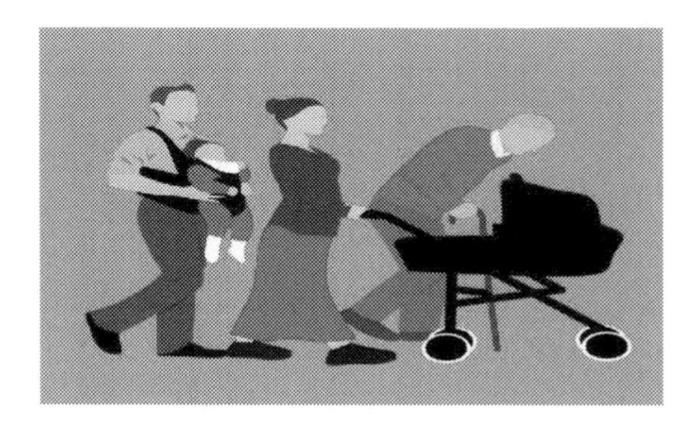

THINKING QUESTIONS:

Challenges of Growing Older:

The challenges that face older people are many in this society. There is much talk about elder abuse, drug abuse in elders, neglect and many other issues as well. Think about these issues and speculate on solutions to these social problems.

The Sandwich Generation:

I was food shopping the other day and in produce I overheard two women talking. They were talking about vacations with one off them saying she was so happy to be finally going on vacation and she was so happy she found a competent sitter. I assumed they were discussing their children. They weren't! They were discussing getting a sitter for their older parents who lived with them while they went on vacation.

The sandwich generation refers to people in their fifties who may still have children at home and who also have a parent living with them who possibly needs care-taking because of ill health. In 2 pages, discuss the issues that could arise in such a situation. How would you go about solving them?

Valuing Older Adults:

In this society we do not value older adults. Why is that? Can you envision a society where age is valued and older people are considered wise? What would have to be different about our society in order for us to experience wisdom in our older people.

The End of Life:

Think about the quality vs the quantity of life. Think how the decline of health affects the psychology of quality of life in older people.

The End of Life

Is there such a thing as The Good Death? What factors do you think are involved in creating an environment conducive for the Good Death to occur? Are there any?

Kubler Ross, who has written extensively in the process of dying, has probably done the most research on how people die. She presented five stages of dying: denial, anger, bargaining, depression, acceptance.

Think about examples of each stage.

What are the challenges faced by older people, such as mental illness, alcohol and drug abuse, dementia, victimization, elder abuse, sexual issues etc. What do you see as some solutions to these Issues?

DEVELOPING EFFECTIVE COMMUNICATION AND LISTENING SKILLS

Early Child

COMMUNICATION STYLES

Your ten year old daughter says to you, "I don't know what's wrong with me. Ginny used to like me, but now she doesn't. She never comes to our house to play and when I go to hers she always plays with Joyce and the two of them play together and have fun and ignore me. I just stand there all by myself. I hate them both."

Which of the following best describes how you would react?

a) Well who would want to play with you? I told you to care about how you look.
b) It's OK honey, I'll play with you, what would you like to do?
c) Why don't you ask both Ginny and Joyce to play here?
d) You're just jealous of Ginny.
e) Come on—let's talk about something more pleasant.
f) Do the kids ever tell you why they don't want to play with you?
g) Other:______________

You receive a note home that your twelve year old son was throwing things and being disruptive in school. He says, "I didn't do anything! The teacher is always picking on me. He hates me!"

Which of the following best describes how you would react?

a) Go for the aspirins.
b) I don't blame the teacher for picking on you, you act like a wild animal!
c) How's it going with your basketball?
d) I agree with you, that the teacher does seem to have it in for you.
e) You shouldn't act like that in school.
f) If I hear one more thing about you getting in trouble in school you will be sorry!
g) Other:_____________

Your eleven year old says to you, "How come I have to take care of the yard and take the garbage out? Johnny's mother doesn't make him do all that stuff? You're not fair! Kids shouldn't have to do that much work. Nobody is made to do as much as I have to do."

Which of the following best describes how you would react?

a) Fine! I'll do it myself.
b) I don't care what other parents do, you have to do the yard work!
c) Look at it this way—your mother needs help around the house.
d) You're a spoiled brat!
e) How many other kids have you talked to about the work they have to do?
f) I used to think that to.

Other:_____________

You have two daughters eight and six years old. Your oldest comes to you saying, "You are always yelling at me, you like Lisa better. You always take her side. I wish I could live with another family."

Which of the following best describes how you would react?

a) Start packing her clothes.
b) You children must learn to get along with one another.
c) That's an immature way to react.
d) Okay, little baby.
e) You really don't want to live with another family.
f) One more statement like that and I'll send you to another family.

Other:_______________

Your five year old son becomes more and more frustrated when he can't get the attention of his mother and father and your two guests after dinner. The four of you are talking intently, renewing your friendship after a long separation. Suddenly you are shocked when your little boy loudly shouts, "You're all a bunch of dirty smelly old stinkbugs. I hate you!"

Which of the following best describes how you would react?

a) Laugh.
b) You must always respect your elders.
c) Look here, Mr. Fresh mouth.
d) Don't talk to our guests that way!
e) That's an immature way to handle your feelings.
f) If you have something you want to say, I suggest you say it nicely.
g) Other:__________________

My Plan for Building Positive Relationships:

My specific concern:

My usual responses:

Talking, lecturing, preaching
Punishing, shaming
Commanding
Other: ____________________
Criticizing, nagging
Threatening, warning
Becoming angry

I would like to change my behavior by doing more:

Listening
Encouraging
Practicing mutual respect

Communicating love
Acknowledging
Mirroring
Using door-openers
Other:

I plan to make changes in the following situation(s):

Questions Parents Never Seem to Get Answers To:

Can you hear me?
What are you, stupid?
But what's wrong with you?
How many times have I told you to stop that?
Why is this happening?
What did I do to deserve this?
Where did you get that idea?
Are you out of your mind?
When are you going to listen?
When are you going to learn?
What did I tell you?
What were you doing while you were out all this time?
How long have you been on that phone?
Don't you have homework?
Shouldn't you be doing your homework?
Where did I go wrong?

PARENT COMMUNICATION

One of the most valuable secrets to building positive relationships with your children is practicing the art of effective communication. In order to fine tune this skill, parents may find it helpful to **identify their own style of communicating** with their children and to **practice alternate methods of communication** where it seems warranted.

Remember: communication is the art of listening to feelings as well as being able to express them.

Suggestions:

1. Ask yourself what areas are of most concern to you in relation to your child.
2. How have you handled communication about these problems in the past?
3. What kind of person do you want your child to be?
4. What qualities do you value and admire in others that you would like to see in your child? (i.e., independence, responsibility, sensitivity to others, productivity, self-confidence...)
5. How might your child acquire these characteristics?

Beware of Static Communication Signals:

1. Messages sent are not the messages received. Nonverbal messages are sent even without verbal messages. It can be helpful to

find out how your child perceives your verbal and nonverbal messages.

2. Mixing fact and opinion.
3. Sending double messages.
4. Forgetting that no two people see things exactly alike.

Avoid Some Typical Parent Responses:

Commanding, warning (threatening), preaching, advising, lecturing, giving solutions, probing, interrogating, judging, criticizing, disagreeing, blaming, interpreting, analyzing, or diagnosing, name-calling, shaming, consoling, distracting, humoring, withdrawing, and giving logical arguments.

TYPICAL PARENT RESPONSES

1. **Commanding**: Telling the child to do something, giving an *order* or *command.*

2. **Warning (threatening)**: Telling the child what the *consequences* will be if something occurs.

3. **Preaching**: Telling the child what *should* or *ought* to be done.

4. **Advising, suggesting, or giving solutions**: Telling the child how to *solve* a problem, giving advice or *suggestions*, or *providing answers.*

5. **Lecturing, teaching or giving logical arguments**: Trying to *influence* the child with facts, *counterarguments, logic,* or you own *opinions.*

6. **Judging, criticizing, disagreeing, blaming**: Making *negative judgment* or *evaluation* of the child.

7. **Praising, agreeing**: Offering a *positive evaluation* or *judgment,* or *agreeing.*

8. **Name-calling, shaming**: Making the child *feel foolish*, putting him/her into a *category, shaming.*

9. **Interpreting, analyzing, or diagnosing**: Telling the child what their *motives* are or *analyzing* why they are doing or saying something, communicating that you have *figured* them out.

10. **Sympathizing, consoling, reassuring, supporting**: Trying to make the child *feel better,* talking them out of their feeling, trying to make their feeling go away, *denying* the strength of their feeling.

11. **Probing, questioning, interrogating**: Trying to find *reasons, motives, causes;* searching for more information to help *you solve the problem.*

12. **Distracting, humoring, withdrawing**: Trying to get the child away from the problem; *withdrawing* from the problem yourself: *distracting* the child, *kidding* them out of it, *pushing* the problem *aside.*

EFFECTS OF TYPICAL PARENT RESPONSES

I feel the need to stop talking or to shut off.
I feel the need to be defensive.
I feel the need to argue, counterattack.
I feel inadequate or inferior.
I feel resentful or angry.
I feel guilty or bad.
I feel I'm being pressured to change – not accepted as I am.
I feel the other person doesn't trust me to solve my problem.
I feel I'm being treated as if I were a child.
I feel I'm no being understood.
I feel my feelings aren't justified.
I feel I've been interrupted.
I feel frustrated.
I feel I'm on the witness stand being cross-examined.
I feel the listener is just not interested.

Recognizing Barriers to Effective Communication

Using the following list of 'barriers,' read each item and write the reason why the parent's message may be ineffective in the space provided.

a) Blaming, judging
b) Providing solutions
c) Sarcasm
d) Venting anger
e) Name-calling
f) Threatening
g) Commanding
h) Preaching

Example: Ten year old left the legos on the floor of the baby's room. **PARENT'S RESPONSE**: "That was so stupid. The baby could have choked." **BARRIER**: A. Blaming, judging

1. Kids fighting over which TV program to watch. **PARENT'S RESPONSE**: "Stop that fighting and turn off the TV right now!" **BARRIER**: _________

2. Daughter arrives home at 2:00 a.m. after agreeing to be home at midnight. Parent has been worried, but is relieved when she finally arrives. **PARENT'S RESPONSE**: "Well, I can see that you cannot be trusted. I am so angry at you. You're grounded for a month." **BARRIER**: ______

3. Twelve year old left gate to back yard open, endangering two year old. **PARENT'S RESPONSE**: "What did you want to do, kill the baby? I'm furious with you."

4. **BARRIER**: ______

5. Teacher sent a not home that eleven year old boy was doing too much loud and 'filthy' talking in class. **PARENT'S RESPONSE**:

"Come in here and explain why you want to embarrass your parents with your dirty mouth." **BARRIER**: ________

6. Child is dawdling and making parent late for an appointment. **PARENT'S RESPONSE**: "I would like for you to be more considerate." **BARRIER**: ________

7. Parent finds home a mess after asking children to keep it clean for company. **PARENT'S RESPONSE**: "I hope you all had a lot of fun this afternoon at my expense." **BARRIER**: ________

8. Parent is repulsed by the sight and odor of child's dirty hands. **PARENT'S RESPONSE**: "Don't you ever wash your hands like other human beings? Get into the bathroom and wash." **BARRIER**: ________

9. Child is acting out to get your attention in front of guests. **PARENT'S RESPONSE**: "You little show off." **BARRIER**: ________

ALTERNATIVE CATEGORIES OF RESPONSE

Silence – Passive Listening:

Listening to a message without verbally responding. Communicates acceptance if the listener gives undivided attention to the speaker.

Simple Acknowledgment:

Verbal non-committal responses to a message.

Door Openers:

Verbal responses which are invitations to say more.

Mirroring:

Repeating messages in a way which conveys that you have heard the speaker.

Active Listening:

Messages which convey back empathetic understanding of a communication. Decoding and feeding back messages:

"Sounds like you feel ____________, because _."

Communicate Your Feelings Using "I" Messages

Use I messages to communicate your positive feelings as well as to communicate things that bother you.

ATTENDING

Five basic skills in attending:

S – SQUARE: Face the child squarely.

O – OPEN: Adopt an open posture. In other words, do not cross your arms.

L – LEAN: Periodically lean toward the child.

E – EYE CONTACT: Maintain good eye contact; however, be aware that it is inappropriate in some cultures to look constantly into a person's eyes.

R – RELAX: Try to relax when you are practicing these skills of attending.

Door Openers

One of the most effective and constructive ways of responding to children's feeling-messages or problem-messages is to use "door openers." Door openers are responses which may invite the speaker to say more. These responses do not communicate the listener's judgments, ideas, or feelings, yet they open the door for the speaker to talk and share their ideas and feelings.

Simple Door Openers:

"I see."
"Oh."
"Mm hmmm."
"How about that."
"Interesting."
"Really."
"You don't say."
"No kidding."
"You did, huh."
"Is that so!"

More Explicit Door Openers:

"Tell me about it."
"Tell me more."
"Tell me the whole story."
"Let's discuss it."
"Shoot, I'm listening."
"I'd like to hear about it."
"I'd be interested in your point of view."
"Would you like to talk about it?"
"Let's hear what you have to say."
"Sounds like you've got something to say about this."
"This seems like something important to you."

Effects of Using Door Openers:

Door openers keep the listener's thoughts and feelings out of the communication process. As a result, the speaker may then feel encouraged to move in closer, open up, and pour out their feelings and ideas. Door openers also convey acceptance of the speaker and respect for him/her as a person. They convey the following messages:

"You have a right to express how you feel."
"I might learn something from you."
"I really want to hear your point of view."
"I am interested in you.
"Your ideas are worthy of being listened to."
"I want to relate to you, get to know you better."
"I respect you as a person with ideas and feelings of your own."

THE TECHNIQUE OF ACTIVE LISTENING

When you use active listening:

- ✓ Listen for the feelings
- ✓ Be willing to take time
- ✓ Avoid "parroting"
- ✓ Respond in various ways
- ✓ Avoid putting your own message in the situation
- ✓ Respect your child's unwillingness to pursue a matter any further
- ✓ Have faith in your child

Active Listening Responses:

- That sounds to me like you are sad about…
- You feel upset about…
- You mean you are afraid of…
- I am not sure I understand. Do you mean you are disappointed that…
- You feel lonely right now because…
- Seems you are sure that…
- You hate that...
- You are irritated with me because…
- That's embarrassing for you to…
- It hurts when you…
- That makes you feel left out when…

- It is totally hopeless right now…
- Wow! That makes you feel proud about…

Don't Use Active Listening When…

- ✓ You have neither the time nor the desire to listen
- ✓ You are angry
- ✓ Your child wants specific information (when will you be home?)
- ✓ Your child does not want to talk about a problem
- ✓ You find it difficult to be separated from your child

COMMUNICATING YOUR FEELINGS TO YOUR CHILDREN

Sending "I" Messages:

There are basically two ways parents can communicate their feeling to their children: they either send *You-messages* or *I-messages.* You messages can be put-downs of children. They may blame, criticize, ridicule, or judge. For example: "You're so rude. Must you constantly interrupt me?"

I-messages simply share how you feel about the consequences a child's behavior produces for you. When parents send I-messages, they take responsibility for their own feelings instead of blaming the child for their feelings. For example, the interrupted parent could respectfully say, "When I'm interrupted I feel discouraged because it seems my opinion is not important."

You-messages tend to reinforce misbehavior or produce ineffective results. I-messages are often unexpected and will frequently "defuse" the situation. Before expressing your feelings of displeasure to the child, consider that it is usually not the child's behavior per se which is displeasing you: but rather how it interferes with your needs or rights.

MODEL:

I-messages generally have three parts, though not necessarily in any particular order:

1. ***Describe the behavior*** which is interfering with you. Just describe, don't blame. Example: "When you don't come home on time..."
2. ***State your feeling*** about the consequence the behavior produces for you.
   Example: "...I worry that something might have happened to you..."
3. ***State the consequence.***
   Example: "...because I don't know where you are."

Constructing an I-Message:

I Feel (state the feeling)
When (state the behavior)
Because (state the consequence)

Constructing an I-Message

Design an I-message for each situation below:

- Your son, who just got his drivers license is backing out of the driveway too fast.
- Your child forgets to feed the dog.
- You have just washed the car. Your child makes a design on it with muddy handprints.
- Your child comes to the table with dirty hands and face.
- Your child prevents you from having a conversation.

Consider a situation that you typically experience.

Whose problem is it?

If appropriate, construct an I-message for the situation.

Activity for the week: Practice using I-messages. Note the results.

EXAMPLES OF "I" MESSAGES:

1. When you are cutting paper and making noise, I really feel annoyed because I am trying to sleep.

2. When you drive and exceed the speed limit, I feel frustrated and scared because it is not safe and may cause an accident.

3. When I am talking on the telephone and you turn up the volume on your stereo, I feel irritated because I cannot hear what is being said.

4. I feel very proud of you when you study for your algebra test because you earned a B+ on the test.

Feeling Words

Below is a list of feeling words. See if you can find other words to add to the list. Be careful with the use of the word *upset*. This is a "catch all" word which may not convey the depth of feeling.

Accepted
Afraid
Angry
Annoyed
Appreciated
Bad
Bored
Bothered
Brave
Comfortable
Confused
Defeated determined
Disappointed
Discouraged
Disrespected
Down
Embarrassed
Foolish
Guilty
Happy
Hurt
Interested
Nervous
Pleased
Proud
Surprised
Trusted
Rejected
Safe

Content
Accepting
Ignored

Good
Excited
Indifferent
Scared
Stressed
Certain
Successful
Undecided
OK
Encouraged
Respected
Up
Proud
Confident
Satisfied
Sad
Loved
Turned off
Relaxed
Irritated
Ashamed
Shocked
Doubted

FINDING THE HIDDEN MESSAGE

Listening For Feelings

Directions: Behind the words, children often communication feelings. Read each statement and try to listen for the feelings being communicated. Discard the content and write the feeling or feelings you heard in the column at the right.

STATEMENT FEELING

STATEMENT	FEELING
1. Dad, guess what? I saved the princess in the video game!	1.
2. Will you hold my hand when we go into nursery school?	2.
3. There's nothing to do around here.	3.
4. I'll never be as good as her. I keep trying and she is still better than me.	4.
5. I can't get all my homework done. My teacher gives too much work. What'll I do?	5.

6. All the kids went to the movies and I don't have anyone.	6.
7. He can go to school by himself and I'm older than he is.	7.
8. I shouldn't have been so mean to her.	8.
9. If I don't tie my shoes it's my business—they're my shoes.	9.
10. Am I doing this right? Is it good enough?	10.
11. I'd like to smack my teacher for making me stay after school. I wasn't the only one who was talking.	11.
12. You don't need to help me. I can do it myself.	12.
13. I'm too dumb to understand math. It's too hard.	13.
14. Leave me alone! You don't care what happens to me anyway. I don't want to talk to you!	14.
15. I don't want to play with him anymore. He's a dope.	15.
16. It's a good thing you guys are my parents.	16.
17. What should I do? I always seem to do the wrong thing.	17.

Points to Remember: Communication & Listening

- Communication begins by listening and indicating you hear the child's feelings and meanings.

- Effective listening involves establishing eye contact and posture which clearly indicate that you are listening.

- Avoid typical parent responses: probing, criticizing, threatening, lecturing…

- Treat your children the way you would treat your best friend.

- Mutual respect involves accepting the child's feelings.

- Reflective listening involves hearing the child's feelings and meanings and stating this is so that child feels understood. It provides a mirror for the child to see himself or herself more clearly.

- Learn to give open responses that accurately state what the other person feels and means.

- Avoid closed responses which ignore the child's feelings, relaying that you have not heard or understood.

- Let your child learn by resisting the impulse to impose your solutions.

BUILDING YOUR CHILD'S SELF ESTTEM AND DEVELOPING ENCOURAGEMENT SKILLS

Constructive Criticism Building Self Esteem?

Building your child's self esteem and feelings of worth is something all parents want for their children. Even though we all want the best for our children and have good intentions, our methods fall short of desired results.

In the following statements, consider the difference between our ideals and what we actually do. Try to think of actions that would be more consistent with the ideals.

Our ideal	What we really do
My child should be responsible and independent.	Force child to perform; do child's work for them.
My child should be respectful and courteous.	Talk down to the child; criticize, distrust, lecture, and punish child.

My child should be happy.	Compliment success, but dwell on mistakes; tell child s/he can do better.
My child should feel adequate, be courageous, and feel good about him/herself.	Do too much for child, implying child is not capable; criticize, make fun of, refuse to allow child to try difficult tasks.

Often our day-to-day relationships with our children do not match our honorable intentions and ideals—and there is a reason for this. Our society has influenced us to be expert at finding fault, to expect the worst, and, in general, to be discouraging toward ourselves and our children.

We do not have to perpetuate this discouraging cycle.

"Mom, I've got the dishes done,"
The girl called from the door.
Her mother smiled and softly said,
"Each day I love you more."

Children deserve a little praise,
For tasks they're asked to do.
If they're to lead a happy life,
So much depends on you.

ATTITUDES AND BEJAVIORS TO ELIMINATE

- **Negative Expectations**: Children internalize the expectations of adults, i.e., when we believe a child won't succeed at a difficult task, we communicate that belief in one way or another.

- **Unreasonably High Standards**: We communicate that we expect them to do better, and let them know that whatever they do, it's never as good as it could have been.

- **Promoting Competition Between Brothers and Sisters**: We praise the successful child while we ignore or criticize the unsuccessful child. Comparisons may be expressed non-verbally: a gesture or a facial expression can trigger competition as effectively as a comment.

- **Over-ambition**: This attitude may influence children not to try anything unless they are certain they will be tops, with the result that they avoid areas in which they see possible failure.

- **Double Standards**: Children recognize that certain socially prescribed rights and privileges, such as driving a car, are restricted to age. But, when parents assume other rights and privileges and deny them to children, this tells the children that they are of less value in the family.

ATTITUDES AND BEHAVIORS THAT ENCOURAGE

- **Accept Your Children As They Are, Not Only As They Could Be**: If we want our children to see themselves as worthwhile persons, we must genuinely accept them as they are, with all their imperfections.

- **Ignore Tattling**: Paying attention to tattling has a very discouraging effect. Children use tattling to make themselves look good or to get even.

- **Be Positive**: An encouraging parent stops using negative comments about a child. When problems arise, the encouraging parent uses methods which are based on respect for the child—listening, I-messages, problem-solving, and natural and logical consequences.

- **Recognize Effort and Improvement As Well As Final Accomplishment**: When parents hold out for achievement—a better grade in math, a neat room at home, some children conclude they are not good enough unless they approximate perfection.

- **Encourage Rather Than Praise**: At first glance, praise and encouragement appear to be the same process. The distinction is that praise is a type of reward and is based on competition. Encouragement, however, is given for effort or improvement. It focuses on the child's assets and strengths as a means for him/her to contribute to the good of all.

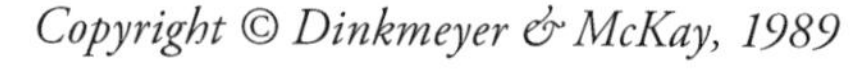
Copyright © Dinkmeyer & McKay, 1989

SEVEN STEPS TO FACILITATE POSITIVE CRITICISM

How do you give your child feedback without sounding mean or nasty? How do you tell them how to improve without them getting defensive or angry? Here are seven easy steps to facilitate positive criticism.

1. Describe what you see the problem to be without attacking the child, judging or moralizing. This will start the conversation without getting off to a discouraging start.

2. Make your feedback as specific as possible. Clear directions focused on the issue not the child. Remember: undesirable behaviors or grades are not the same as undesirable children.

3. Give feedback when the child is most ready to hear it. Find a time when there are few distractions, or when other activities will not have to be sacrificed, unless immediate attention is appropriate.

4. Check to see if your child understands what you are saying. Ask them to repeat or put it in their own words to see if it makes sense to them. They may feel your feedback is a personal attack. For example, asking them to perform a task a certain way may be interpreted as "You hate the way I do things!" Be sure to remain calm, repeat and then reassure them of what you said and intended to mean.

5. Give feedback in small doses, avoid overwhelming your child. This will facilitate participation and cooperation.

6. Use "I" statements and focus on how you think and feel to prevent defensive reactions.

7. If your child feels you are being mean or unreasonable, ask a neutral person for feedback on the situation. Accept their constructive criticism and make suitable changes. This way the child's feelings are not being ignored, and you can make appropriate modifications when necessary.

HOW TO ENCOURAGE DEVELOPMENT OF HEALTHY SELF-ESTEEM

- Encourage good communication
- Use "I" messages
- Supply parental warmth, love, unconditional acceptance
- Have realistic expectations.
- Give encouragement
- Set definite limits on acceptable behavior.
- Respect the child.
- Teach decision-making skills
- Be a positive role model
- Place trust and give responsibility
- Be aware of strengths and assets
- Self-praise

101 WAYS TO PRAISE A CHILD

* Wow * Way To Go * Super * You're Special * Outstanding * Excellent * Great * Good * Neat * Well Done * Remarkable * I Knew You Could Do It * I'm Proud Of You * Fantastic * Super Star * Nice Work * Looking Good * You're On Top Of It * Beautiful * Now You're Flying * You're Catching On * Now You've Got It * You're Incredible * Bravo * You're Fantastic * Hurray For You * You're On Target * You're On Your Way * How Nice * How Smart * Good Job * That's Incredible * Hot Dog * Dynamite * You're Beautiful * You're Unique * Nothing Can Stop You Now * Good For You * I like You * You're A Winner * Remarkable Job * Beautiful Work * Spectacular * You're Spectacular * You're A Darling * You're Precious * Great Discovery * You've Discovered The Secret * You Figured It Out * Fantastic Job * Hip, Hip, Hurray * Bingo * Magnificent * Marvelous * Terrific * You're Important * Phenomenal * You're Sensational * Super Work * Creative Job * Super Job * Fantastic Job * Exceptional Performance * You're A Real Trooper * You Are Responsible * You Are Exciting * You Learned It Right * What An Imagination * What A Good Listener * You Are Fun * You're Growing Up * You Tried Hard * You Care * Beautiful Sharing * Outstanding Performance * You're A Good Friend * I Trust You * You're Important * You Mean A Lot To Me * You Make Me Happy * You Belong * You've Got A Friend * You Make Me Laugh * You Brighten My Day * I Respect You * You Mean The World To Me * That's Correct * You're A Joy * You're A Treasure * You're Wonderful * You're Perfect * Awesome * A+ Plus Job * You're The Best * A Big Hug * A Big Kiss * Say I Love You!

P.S. Remember, a smile is worth a thousand words.

POINTS TO REMEMBER ENCOURAGEMENT

Building Your Child's Confidence And Feelings Of Worth

- Encouragement is the process of focusing on your children's assets and strengths in order to build their self-confidence and feelings of worth.
- Focus on what is good about the child or the situation. See the positive.
- Accept your children as they are. Don't make your love and acceptance dependent on their behavior.
- Have faith in your children so they can come to believe in themselves.
- Let your children know their worth. Recognize improvement and effort, not just accomplishment.
- Respect your children. It will lay the foundation of their self-respect.

- Praise is reserved for things well done. It implies a spirit of competition. Encouragement is given for effort or improvement. It implies a spirit of cooperation.

- The most powerful forces in human relationships are expectations. We can influence a person's behavior by changing our expectations of the person.

- Lack of faith in children helps them to anticipate failure.

- Standards that are too high invite failure and discouragement.

- Avoid subtle encouragement of competition between brothers and sisters.

- Avoid using discouraging words and actions.

- Avoid tacking qualifiers onto your words of encouragement. Don't "give with one hand and take away with the other."

- The sounds of encouragement are words that build feelings of adequacy…

  "I like the way you handled that."
  "I know you can handle it."
  "I appreciate what you did."
  "It looks as if you worked very hard on that."
  "You're improving."

Be generous with them.

CREATING STRATEGIES FOR APPROPRIATE CONSEQUENCES

Discipline

How do you define discipline? What does discipline mean to you? What is the goal of discipline? What is it we hope to accomplish when we discipline children?

We often hear people say, "Spare the Rod, Spoil the Child," when referring to discipline. What does that mean?

Discipline comes from the word "disciple" which means to teach. Children are expected to behave a certain way yet they are not told what is expected of them. The rod that is so often mentioned does not mean that you have to spank the child. Rather, the rod refers to the staff the shepherds used to gently move the sheep in the direction they wanted them to go.

That is exactly what is meant when discipline and children are discussed.

The goal is to help children move in the direction that parents think is right and appropriate.

Another goal is to help children reach the level of self-discipline. Parents are not always going to be with the child, and you want children to "behave," whether you are present or absent.

When should discipline occur? Before the behavior/misdeed? After the behavior/misdeed?

Discipline should occur before the behavior/misdeed. The critical issue is teaching the child about acceptable behaviors so he/she will know in advance how to behave. This does not negate that at times children will misbehave. The difference is they will know internally that they are doing something wrong and move to correct the behavior sometimes even before parents can intervene.

Discipline Relates to Self-Concept:

Appropriate disciplinary measures fuels positive self-concept; aids in mental stability; encourages healthy growth and development.

Remember the rights of children? More specifically, to maintenance: food, clothing, shelter; to protection; to emotional security; to education; to medical care; to privacy; etc.

What is the relationship between these rights and discipline?

When disciplining children bear in mind the objective is to protect rather than violate those rights.

PUNISHMENT

How is punishment similar or different from discipline? What doe punishment mean to you? How do you define it?

Punishment is a negative consequence; it occurs after a behavior; it aims to stop the behavior or is a deterrent.

What are some examples of punishment?

Do these protect the rights of children? Do they engender positive self-concept?

Why punishment doesn't work and what does:

- ✓ Punishment can be punitive and may increase rage, revenge, defiance, and guilt, while decreasing introspection.
- ✓ Deprivation is easy but not always appropriate.
- ✓ Hitting increases guilt for the parent while teaching the child that when one is angry, one hits.

Discipline by appropriate consequences:

- Teaches alternatives to punishment
- Increases children's understanding of appropriate behavior
- Corrects misbehavior and discourages repetition of misbehavior
- Does not use punitive statements, is relevant to the action, and makes sense to the child
- Uses "I" messages to communicate anger and disappointment while giving the child a chance to make amends
- May put the child in a position of problem solver thereby building upon problem solving skills

Why Not Use Physical Force When Your Child Misbehaves:

- ✓ Even if hitting her makes her stop misbehaving for that minute, it teaches her it's OK to hit and yell when upset and angry
- ✓ Physical punishment, even the lightest slap, can harm a child
- ✓ Hitting teaches the child fear rather than self-control
- ✓ Hitting teaches the child that it is OK to hurt and be hurt by those you love
- ✓ Hitting teaches that problems get resolved through violence

ALTERNATIVES TO HITTING CHILDREN:

- ✓ STOP AND THINK! STEP BACK OR SIT DOWN
- ✓ TAKE A FEW DEEP BREATHS—EXHALE SLOWLY
- ✓ COUNT TO 20 OR 100—WHATEVER IT TAKES YOU TO RELAX
- ✓ PHONE A FRIEND OR RELATIVE—TALK ABOUT ANYTHING OR ASK FOR HELP
- ✓ WRITE A LIST ABOUT ALL THE THINGS YOU LIKE ABOUT YOUR CHILD/ABOUT YOURSELF
- ✓ PUT ON A FAVORITE RECORD, CD, OR RADIO STATION/READ A MAGAZINE OR BOOK
- ✓ EXPLAIN TO THE CHILD WHY YOU ARE ANGRY IF THE CHILD IS OLD ENOUGH TO UNDERSTAND
- ✓ ASK YOURSELF WHY YOU ARE GOING TO SMACK YOUR CHILD
- ✓ ASK YOURSELF WILL SMACKING YOUR CHILD MAKE THINGS BETTER

CONSEQUENCES OF HITTING:

The goal in raising children is to enable them, first, to discover who they want to be, and then to become people who can be satisfied with themselves and their way of life. Eventually, they ought to be able to do in their lives whatever seems important, desirable, and worthwhile to them to do; to develop relationships with other people that are constructive, satisfying, mutually enriching; and to bear up well under the stresses and hardships they will unavoidably encounter during their life. In this regard, parents are not just foremost teachers, they are those by whom and through whom children orient themselves wit the world around them.

Children have a need for attachment and parents can build on their need in order to promote the child's self-control and a lasting inner commitment to be a discipline person. Discipline cannot be forced on another person. Any discipline worth acquiring cannot be beaten into anyone; indeed, such effort is contrary to the very ideas of healthy growth and development. Hitting teaches children fear, poor self-concept, feelings of revenge, and the idea that it's okay to hit those you love. It does not teach children to obey rules, be careful, make wise choices, or have inner control.

Hitting, even the threat of hitting, often teaches children fear. Children who learn to fear their parents often learn to fear other adults as well. The sheer difference in size between parents and children can be frightening. When parents threaten or use their physical superiority as a form of punishment, young children realize there is no way they could ever win. Their safety is literally at the mercy of the angry parent.

The self-concept and self-esteem of children develop from how they are treated. Children who are constantly threatened or hit learn that they are not worthy people, are not loved, and are not wanted. Nobody ever feels good after being hit. The more frequent the hitting, the more constant the feelings of inadequacy. In addition, many studies indicate children who have been hit exhibit a high degree of anxiety as well as feelings of helplessness.

Children who have been repeatedly hit often want to seek revenge. Getting back is a common result of spanking. Young children who can't hit back may seek revenge in other ways, such as breaking something that belongs to the parents, writing on the walls, or stealing. Studies have generally shown that the most punished children tend to be the most aggressive. They have learned that hitting is the way to deal with anger and frustration.

In years of research conducted by this writer in assessing the parenting and child rearing attitudes of thousands of teenagers and adults, it was establish that a remarkable transmission of attitudes is passed on from parents to children.

Utilizing the *Adult Adolescent Parenting Inventory (AAPI)*, attitudes regarding four specific parenting behaviors were assessed:

- Expectations parents have for children
- An ability to be empathic to the needs of children
- The belief in the use of corporal punishment as a means of discipline
- The definition of family roles

Not surprisingly, adolescents who had been repeatedly spanked and who were identified as abused had grossly inappropriate developmental expectations of children; lacked an empathic awareness of childrens' needs; believe strongly in the use of corporal punishment as a means of disciplining children; and were confused about family roles, expressing reversals between parents and children. The tragedy of these findings is that these attitudes were similar to the attitudes of known adult child abusers.

These findings have been validated throughout the country in a number of settings. Children who have been repeatedly spanked develop views about parenting and child rearing that, if not replaced with more nurturing attitudes, may lead to abusive parenting and child rearing attitudes.

INSTEAD OF PUNISHMENT—DISCIPLINE

✓ ***Express your feelings strongly—without attacking character.***
I'm furious that my new tool was left outside to rust in the rain!"

✓ ***State your expectations.***
"I expect my tools to be returned after they've been borrowed."

✓ ***Show the child how to make amends.***
"What this tool needs now is a little steel wool and a lot of elbow grease."

- ✓ ***Give the child a choice.***

  "You can borrow my tools and return them or you can give up the privilege of using them. You decide."

- ✓ ***Take action.***

  Lock the tool box.

- ✓ ***Problem solve.***

  - "What can we work out so that you can use my tools when you need them and so that I'll be sure they're there when I need them?"

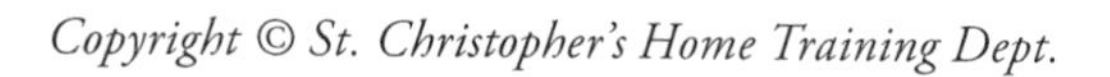

POSITIVE DISCIPLINE

There is no magic formula for discipline, no tried and true method that works in every situation. There are always at least several helpful methods that will be effective, depending on the child's mood, our own, and what's happening at the moment. Once we commit ourselves to using the positive methods and practice them daily, they become second nature. Here are some to try:

- ✓ Don't assume a child knows your rules. Make expectations clear.
- ✓ Redirect. "The chair isn't for jumping on. Jump on that mat."
- ✓ Be encouraging. "I know you can put the toys away on time." This gets cooperation, whereas a negative remark, "You never get your jobs done," brings more misbehavior.
- ✓ Involve children in decisions. Ask them to help think of a solution to the problem.
- ✓ Give choice, "Play indoors with the quiet toy or outside with the ball." Children are more agreeable when they've some say.
- ✓ Sometimes, there is no choice: "You'd like to stay up later, but 8:00 o'clock is your bedtime."
- ✓ Use humor. It lightens everyone's mood. "Abra-ka-dabra and ;your pajamas are on."
- ✓ Have a child take responsibility. If he has hurt his sister's feelings, ask him to think of a way to make her feel better.
- ✓ Appreciate good behavior and notice improvements. Your praise is the child's incentive to keep it up!

When words aren't winning a child's cooperation, don't take a punitive stance. Turn to helpful actions:

- ✓ Remove any object or game the child is misusing until she's ready to use it correctly.
- ✓ Remove a privilege that's being misused. But as soon as the child is ready to handle it responsibly, return the privilege. This shows you're on the child's side. When he's capable of behaving correctly, you're glad of it.

When we set limits in a positive way, we help children to grow in a nurturing, supportive environment. We eliminate children's fear of adults, and put trust in its place.

APPROACHES TO DISCIPLINE

Most of us automatically use the methods of discipline that we are most familiar with—what our parents used to discipline us.

However, discipline is taught in several ways:

- Setting an example by your own behavior
- Allowing a child to make mistakes and helping him/her to recover
- Letting the child know that you have positive expectations for him/her which s/he can realistically meet
- Teaching him/her about cause and effect
- Helping him/her to live and work in a group
- Emphasizing with him/her the things s/he has done right as well

HINTS:

Prevention
Love abundantly
Discipline constructively
Be consistent
Be clear
Administer in private
Be reasonable and understanding
Be flexible
Discourage continued dependency

Be authoritative
Spend time together
Really listen
Develop mutual respect
Be realistic

RULES FOR CORRECTIVE MEASURE:

- ✓ Relate the consequence to the offense
- ✓ Make consequences by psychologically correct for the child
- ✓ Remember, no corporal punishment
- ✓ Give logical reasons for the consequences
- ✓ Admit your mistakes
- ✓ Do not take remedial action when you are angry
- ✓ Be truthful
- ✓ Try to find out the underlying causes—all behavior has meaning
- ✓ Do not expect him/her to tell you why s/he did something
- ✓ Be encouraging and praising
- ✓ Remember, all feelings are acceptable
- ✓ Try to say "yes"
- ✓ Be disciplined yourself

APPROACHES TO DISCIPLINE

Techniques For Pre-Teens

Realistic Expectations:

- ✓ Behavior may mimic adolescence.
- ✓ Girls may be more mature in their thinking and in their concerns than boys.
- ✓ Both boys and girls may be moody and involved with the expression of feelings.
- ✓ The preteen exhibits the growth of abstract logic, but is not consistent with it.
- ✓ The preteen may exhibit beginning attempts to break away.
- ✓ A sense of ethics should be well developed.
- ✓ Peer pressure may be more potent that loyalty to the family.

Parental Goals:

- ✓ Make sure your child has had a substantial education in sexual matters.
- ✓ Develop negotiating skills.
- ✓ Help your child develop good judgment and civic responsibility.
- ✓ Protect your child's physical and emotional health.

Techniques:

- Handle sensitive matters delicately. Try to avoid very harsh punishments and empty threats.
- Provide clear guidelines for sexual and social conduct.
- Be a model for restraint and civilization.
- Provide ample education regarding dangers of drugs, alcohol and smoking.
- Give your child handy excuses to withstand peer pressure so he can avoid drugs, alcohol and smoking.
- Give your child opportunities for making judgments.
- Make it clear that you will not condone cheating, lying, stealing, vandalism, rude and fresh behavior or the taking of drugs, alcohol, or tobacco.
- Allow your child to experience logically related punishments; if those are impossible, them make it clear that privileges will be removed or the child will be grounded for infractions.
- Make limits clear.
- Take your child's opinions seriously. Do not patronize a competing viewpoint.

POINTS TO REMEMBER:

1. Effective discipline helps children learn self-control and cooperation.
2. Reward and punishment are not effective methods of discipline. They teach children to expect an adult to be responsible for their behavior.
3. In selecting an appropriate method, it's important to consider a child's developmental level.
4. Effective methods of discipline are:
    - Distracting the child
    - Ignoring misbehavior when appropriate
    - Structuring the environment

- Controlling the situation, not the child
- Involving the child through choices and consequences
- Planning time for loving
- Letting go
- Increasing your consistency
- Noticing positive behavior
- Excluding the child with a time out

5. Use natural and logical consequences to give choices to a child. Natural consequences result from going against the laws of nature. Logical consequences are the result of going against the rules of social cooperation.
6. Logical consequences
   - Express the rules of social living
   - Are related to the misbehavior
   - Separate the deed from the doer
   - Are concerned with what will happen now, not with past behavior
   - Are given in a friendly way
   - Permit choice

GUIDELINES FOR USING LOGICAL CONSEQUENCES:

- When a child makes a decision, let the decision stand—for the moment. Later give the child another opportunity to cooperate.
- Increase the amount of time for the consequences each time the same misbehavior happens.
- When you give a child a choice, phrase the choice respectfully.
- Respect the child's choice.
- Say as little as possible and avoid nagging or threatening.
- Make it clear when there is no choice.
- Keep hostility out of consequences.

7. Spending some quality time each day with your child is good for your relationship and can help prevent behavior problems.
8. Too much protection, permissiveness, or demands for obedience will prevent children from becoming independent.
9. A time-out is a form of logical consequences. Use it as a last resort, when other methods haven't worked.
10. Choose a relaxed time to teach skills and make the training fun.

TAKE A MOMENT TO LISTEN

Denis Waithy

FROM SEEDS OF GREATNESS

Praise their smallest triumphs.
Praise their smallest deeds.
Tolerate their chatter.
Amplify their laughter.
Take a moment to listen today
To what your children are trying to say;
Listen today, whatever you do,
And they will come back and listen to you.

EMOTIONS AND AVOIDING DAILY BATTLES

What Would You Do?

Directions:

Choose the response which is closest to what you might do in each given situation. Talk it over among your group and decide upon a choice you can all agree on. If none of the choices are your preferred response, fill in the choice for **"other"** and try to suggest an alternate response.

1. Your teen has come home and announced that she was sent down to the principals office for talking too much in class. She states that she *"hates that **old** @?**$"* and her *"lousy teacher"*. You respond by:

   a. getting an aspirin.
   b. saying "You what? You were sent to the principals office!"
   c. saying "Well that should teach you."
   d. saying "Now then, your teacher isn't that bad is he?"
   e. saying "Sweetheart, you have to learn some self control."
   f. saying "You'd better learn to adjust to all kinds of teachers."
   g. Other__________

2. Your 15-year old announces the following at dinner: "School doesn't mean anything. All you do is learn a lot of garbage that doesn't do you any good. There's a lot of other ways to get ahead in this world and I don't need no college!" Your response is to:

   a. say "You feel that way because you're not doing well in school."
   b. say "You're not thinking clearly."
   c. say "College can be *the* most wonderful experience you'll ever have."
   d. say "What will you do if you don't go to college?".
   e. tell him/her to wait a couple of years before deciding to go to college.
   f. correct his/her grammar.
   g. Other___________

3. Your 13 year old complains to you about a young sister. *"Will you please keep her away from my stuff. She keeps taking my things!"* Your response is to say:

   a. "She's only a kid. There's no reason to get crazy!"
   b. "Why don't you just put your things away?"
   c. "If you'd stop teasing her she wouldn't bother you!"
   d. "Stop complaining!"
   e. "You're acting like a baby your self"
   f. "OK, I'll tell her."
   g. Other_____________

4. Your 16 year old insists on going to a party until 2 a.m. The crowd that will be there has a horrible reputation, but your teen claims that "everyone else is allowed to go". Your reaction is to:

   a. Tell him to ask his mother (father).
   b. Explain that he has poor taste in friends.

c. Warn that he had better not go if he know what's good for him.
d. Tell him to make new friends.
e. Lock him in his room.
f. Argue that not everyone is going to the party.
g. Other__________________

5. Your 14 year old son sadly states that he can't make friends at school. He claims that the other students are all in their own groups. "Most of them won't even talk to me," he states. You respond by saying:

a. "It can't be all that bad."
b. "All kids go through this sometime."
c. "You're just feeling sorry for yourself."
d. "That's not true. You have plenty of opportunities to make friends."
e. "What are you doing wrong?"
f. "Why don't you try advertising?"
g. Other__________________

6. Your 12 year old comes home complaining and swearing. Her comments are vulgar and insulting. You react by:

a. Swearing back.
b. Warning that one more statement like that and you'll "wash her mouth out with soap".
c. Saying, "Where did you get the idea that you could talk to me like that? When I was your age I would never have spoken like that to one of my parents."
d. Saying, "You have a filthy mouth!"
e. Telling her that she is only saying that to get at you.
f. Putting a towel over your eyes and saying, "Help me Lord!"
g. Other__________________

DEALING WITH NEGATIVE EMOTIONS:

- ✓ Construct plans for dealing with situations that evoke negative emotions.
  - o The expression of negative emotions is in large part determined by gender and/or culture.
  - o Unfortunately, the United States has a limited repertoire for languaging and/or dealing these emotions.
  - o Feeling persecuted, vengeful, rejected, disappointed, blaming or condemning others, and attitudes of self-righteousness may effect the way in which individuals deal with anger.

- ✓ Learn to express anger appropriately and/or use reasoning, logical consequences, and cooperative strategies for parenting.
  - o Inappropriate expression of anger can be damaging in children's experience.
  - o Seize opportunities to clearly demonstrate positive emotions to children where possible.
  - o Emotions of parents and children flow in reciprocal, escalating cycles (i.e., positive emotions elicit cooperation and positive emotional responses, while negative emotions elicit resistance and negative emotional responses and so on).

- ✓ Express anger in a way that informs children that their actions are inappropriate or unacceptable.
  - o Emotions are linked with reactions (and therefore parenting skills).
    - ▪ Weak emotional responses from parents may not convey clear messages.
    - ▪ Strong emotional responses can be problematic when parents' reactions are incompatible with more appropriate reactions for child-rearing.

      For example: Angry parents may avoid, criticize, or punish children at moments when children instead need support, instruction, or clarification.

- ✓ Utilize communication and listening skills.
    - o Be assertive, but avoid using "I-messages" as angry "you-messages" said in a different way.
    - o When parents send hostile messages, it is very difficult for children to interpret them as non-threatening.

- ✓ It is helpful to remember that emotions are transient.
    - o Emotions can only be maintained by an individual for a time.

Other suggestions:

Stress-inoculation, self-instructional training, relaxation-desensitization, cathartic expression, assertiveness training, developing problem solving skills, and exploring the meaning of stimuli which elicit anger.

DEALING WITH YOUR EMOTIONS

Emotions can be created from a thought or belief. For example, we may believe that life should or must be a certain way: then we become upset (sometimes overly upset) when life doesn't meet with our expectations. If you hold some of the following beliefs, you may see negative events as catastrophes rather than simple annoyances, and you may blame yourself, others, or life for negative situations. You may even believe that you cannot handle a situation, even though a more useful belief would be that you can handle it (even if you don't like it).

I should be perfect.
I should be right
I should be the best
I should make a good impression.
I should win.
People should give me my own way.
I should succeed.
People should recognize my contribution.
I should always be in control.
Life should be fair.
I should please everyone.
Life should be easy.

A key to changing these negative patterns of thinking is to decide that there is no reason why things should be as we want them. If we recognize this belief, we may become annoyed or disappointed, but we won't experience these situations as catastrophes.

If you find yourself strongly upset, see if you can find a "**SHOULD**" belief that is contributing to your distress. If so, to change your feelings you may want to try following these steps:

- ✓ Decide to look at the situation as unfortunate, not as catastrophic.
- ✓ Decide to accept imperfections, not to blame.
- ✓ Decide you can take what life dishes out.
- ✓ Decide there's no rational reason why any person or situation should follow your orders.

Modified from Dinkmeyer & McKay (1982) Systemic Training for Effective Parenting. Minnesota. American Guidance Service.

DEALING WITH ANGER

What do I get angry about?

- ✓ The illusion of helplessness and being out of control.
- ✓ The illusion that children's misbehavior reflects badly on us.
- ✓ The painful acknowledgment that children can enrage us.
- ✓ Re-experiencing the hurt of old wounds.
- ✓ Not getting our needs met.
- ✓ Unfulfilled expectations

What can be done?

- ✓ Exit the scene and make amends later. Inform children that the anger is not permanent.
- ✓ Don't make decisions when angry or highly agitated.
- ✓ Take a time-out for yourself, cool down, and then make decisions from a more rational place.
- ✓ Remember the goal is to change behavior, not to hurt.

Talk about your feelings. Tell people when things bother you.

Use "I" messages rather than attack.

Use brief messages in an authoritative, nonjudgmental, tone of voice.

Vent anger in appropriate ways.

Find a physical way to release your energy, like hitting a pillow, running or doing push-ups.

Sit on your hands, count to 10, and breath deeply.

Make your own "self-talk tape." Use anger as the signal to press "PLAY".

Keep "self focused" rather than "other focused." Assertion rather than aggression or passivity.)

Try changing the situations that make you angry.

Formulate plans for dealing with anger in the future. In detail, visualize the success of the plans.

When children express their anger, try to be empathic.

Use active listening, mirroring, suggest time-out to cool down or other appropriate methods for venting and controlling anger.

Remember: How you deal with your anger provides a model for your children as well.

JUST FOR YOU

Relieving Your Stress:

Being a parent is a twenty-four-hour-a-day, seven-day-a-week job. It's no wonder, then, if we find ourselves under stress some of the time! Stress is a physical and emotional response to events we find upsetting. There are several ways to ease and handle stress that you may wish to use in the coming weeks:

- ✓ Use deep breathing for about fifteen seconds. Let your breathing pace itself—don't force it. Practice silently saying "calm" as you breathe in and "down" as you breathe out until you begin to feel relaxed.

- ✓ Use positive self-talk. Say simple, upbeat statements: "Be calm." "Take it easy." "You're okay."

- ✓ Prepare yourself for a situation you think might be stressful. Take a few deep breaths and talk to yourself before facing the situation.

- ✓ Think of a situation as an opportunity or a challenge, rather than as something stressful or something you can't handle.

- ✓ Everyday, accept yourself and take time to concentrate on your positive qualities. Make self-affirming statements: "I'm capable." "I'm worthwhile." "I make my own decisions."

- ✓ Take a few moments now to jot down some affirming statements about your positive beliefs and behaviors.

Begin practicing stress reduction this week.

Modified from Dinkmeyer & McKay (1982) Systemic Training for Effective Parenting. Minnesota. American Guidance Service.

WHAT INDIVIDUALS GET ANGRY ABOUT AND WHY

- ✓ Beliefs about ourselves and others can effect our emotional state.
- ✓ Parent's emotions are typically effected by their wants and needs.
- ✓ Emotions are largely automatic
- ✓ *Thus, parents might consider the idea that some of their reactions to children's behavior may be related to an unconscious search for "wholeness" and/or re-experiencing situations which stimulate the hurt of their own "wounds" from childhood.*
- ✓ Anger can be considered a reaction to experiencing other emotions.
- ✓ *For example, feelings of hurt, disappointment, frustration, helplessness, and loss of control, have been known to trigger angry responses.*
- ✓ Individuals may experience anger if they believe that they:
  - o Lack parenting skills
  - o Are incompetent, or
  - o Are unable to cope with or control events
- ✓ Individuals may use anger as a way to control others.
- ✓ Anger may represent a lack of self-focus and emotional responsibility.

- ✓ Anger may be an evolutionary protective mechanism.

- ✓ *Thus, while anger may prepare persons to perceive and remove obstructions, it may also interfere with empathic concern for children.*

- ✓ Anger may arise in conjunction with situational pressures.
(i.e., work, difficulties in relationships with spouses, stress) – all of which contribute to parents' negative attributions about their functioning as parents.

AVOIDING DAILY BATTLES

- ✓ Decrease reactivity, commands, criticism and lectures, which invite defiance.
- ✓ Increase cooperative statements (i.e., "When…", "As soon as…")
- ✓ Increase effective communication
  - o Listen empathically and acknowledging feelings.
  - o Talk less – i.e., using one word reminders).
  - o Decrease use of "You" statements and begin using "I" messages.
- ✓ Allow children to learn from logical consequences.
- ✓ Allow opportunities for children to become problem solvers.
  - o Provide choices within limits.
  - o Provide time for family consultations and meetings; for agreements.
- ✓ Learning to Let Go
  - o Give children opportunities to make decisions.
  - o Decrease controls to increase autonomy in appropriate situations.
  - o Allow children a voice in choosing clothing, food, how to spend free time, when to do class work, etc.
- ✓ Be supportive and encouraging, even if children don't succeed.

HANDLING CONFLICT IN ADULT RELATIONSHIPS

Exploring alternatives can be used to address problems with children. It can also be used when a conflict occurs with a spouse, a friend, or a relative. You can use the steps for exploring alternatives to negotiate agreements.

- ✓ Understand the problem.
- ✓ Use brainstorming to find possible solutions (alternatives).
- ✓ Consider the suggested solutions.
- ✓ Choose a solution.
- ✓ Make or obtain a commitment to a solution and set a time to evaluate.

Rudolph Dreikurs, a psychiatrist and author, identified four important principles for handling conflict:

- ✓ Maintain mutual respect. Avoid fighting or giving in. Use reflective listening and "I" messages.
- ✓ Identify the real issue. You may be discussing money or sharing responsibilities. But what's being discussed is seldom the real issue. Many times the real issue is who is right, who will be in charge, or fairness. You can say something like, "It seems to me we're both interested in being right. I wonder how this will help us solve the problem."
- ✓ Change the agreement. In a conflict, the persons involved have made an agreement to quarrel. You can change the agreement

by changing your own behavior. Be willing to compromise if necessary.

✓ Invite participation in decision making. An agreement comes when both persons suggest solutions and settle on one both are willing to accept. If this doesn't happen, all yau can do is state your intentions: 'Since we aren't willing to find a solution acceptable to both of us, the I choose" Your intentions simply tell what you will do—not what the other person does.

If you have a conflict in your adult relationships you'd like to resolve, decide how to use the steps for exploring alternatives and the principles of conflict resolution to handle the conflict. How will you begin the discussion?

A WORD ABOUT RELATIVES AND FRIENDS

Sometimes others don't understand your child-rearing methods and may interfere with them You can recognize their feelings and state your reasons for your actions. ("I understand you're uncomfortable with the way I'm raising ____________, but I find this works for me.") You may have to confront others and give them choices ("I don't agree with treating ______________ that way. It's discouraging. If you choose to continue, we'll stop visiting for a while until you and I can come to an agreement."). This may be hard for you to do, but you have to decide what's best for your child.

Adapted from Dinkmeyer & Mckay, 1989; R. Dreikurs, 1973.

WHOSE PROBLEM IS IT?

The Concept of Problem Ownership:

Effective responses to parent-child concerns depend upon who owns the problem. For example, if the parent owns the problem it is helpful for the parent to incorporate the use of "I-messages": if the child owns the problem, it is helpful for parents to mobilize listening skills. You can determine who owns the problem by asking yourself these questions when something happens:

1. Who does this problem really effect?
2. Who is having a problem with whom?
3. Whose responsibility is it to take care of this problem?

Examples:

- A parent is trying to watch a favorite TV show and the children are in the same room laughing and teasing each other. The parent has the problem: how to stop the behavior so the parent can watch the show. The children are not concerned with the interruption. They may simply want attention. The fact that the parent is busy is the parent's problem. The parent has to handle the situation.

- A child is having difficulties with a friend. The child's problem in no way affects the parent or interferes with the parent's rights as a person. It's up to the child to handle the problem (unless there is a danger to the child or someone else).

Summary:

In every parent-child relationship three situations may occur:

1. The child owns the problem because there is some obstacle which prevents him/her satisfying a need.
2. There is no problem since the child is satisfying his/her own needs without interfering with a parent satisfying their needs.
3. The parent owns the problem because the child is satisfying his/her needs, but his/her behavior is interfering with the parent's satisfying a need of their own.

PROBLEM LIST

Directions:

In the space provided, mark a "P" if the parent owns the problem and a "C" if the child owns it.

Child misbehaves in public.
Fighting with brothers and sisters.
Leaving belongings around the house.
Misbehavior at school
Homework is not done
Not going to bed on time
Uncooperative during the morning routine
Messing up the kitchen
Misbehavior at the dinner table
Not getting along with peers
Coming home late
Writing on walls
Borrowing the car without permission
Hanging out with the 'wrong' crowd
Child unhappy about assigned chores

POINTS TO REMEMBER

✓ Emotions serve a purpose. They provide the energy for us to act.

- ✓ Take responsibility for your own emotions and encourage your teen to do the same.

  Typical negative emotions of teenagers include:

  anger
  apathy
  boredom
  sadness and depression
  guilt
  fear and anxiety
  stress

- ✓ You can help your teen handle negative emotions through listening, encouragement, and involving the teen in constructive family responsibilities.

- ✓ To redirect our teens' misbehavior we must change not only how we respond, but what we feel as well.

- ✓ We create our own emotions by holding certain beliefs about things that happen in our lives.

- ✓ We catastrophize by translating our preferences into needs.

- ✓ When we make demands on life, we are involved in irrational thinking.

- Some typical irrational beliefs of parents regarding teens are:

  - ✓ To be a good parent I must (**should**) have the approval of everyone in the community.
  - ✓ I should (**must**) be competent in all aspects of parenting.
  - ✓ Things should turn out the way I want them to.
  - ✓ People are victims of circumstances and should not try to change what can't be changed.

  - ✓ I should take the responsibility for my teenager's behavior. If I were a more effective parent, my teen would always be well behaved.

- ✓ Your responses to your teen's misbehavior are created by what you tell yourself about the misbehavior. You can change your responses by changing your thinking (your belief).

- Irrational responses can be changed by using the following strategies:

  - ✓ Admit your feelings, accept yourself, and make a commitment to change.
  - ✓ Identify the purpose of your negative emotions.
  - ✓ Watch your tone of voice.
  - ✓ Watch your nonverbal behavior.
  - ✓ Distract yourself.
  - ✓ Avoid your first impulse and do the unexpected.
  - ✓ Learn to relax.
  - ✓ Use your sense of humor.
  - ✓ Work directly on changing your irrational beliefs.

LET ME BE A CHILD

Let me tell you when I'm feeling bad or angry.
And let me know that even on my worst days, you still like me.
Let me dream.
Share my joy when my dreams come true.
Share my tears when they don't.
Let me laugh.
Let me play.
And most of all let me be a child.
Anonymous

Printed in the United States
By Bookmasters